Page 6

Page 15

Page 18

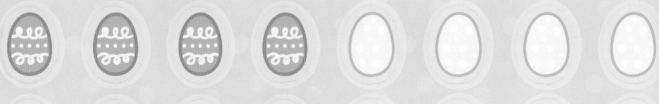

Peppa's Egg-citing Easter!

By Courtney Carbone

A GOLDEN BOOK · NEW YORK

This book is based on the TV series Peppa Pig. Peppa Pig is created by Neville Astley and Mark Baker.
Peppa Pig © Astley Baker Davies Ltd/Entertainment One UK Ltd 2003.

www.peppapig.com

ISBN 978-0-593-12266-2
rhcbooks.com
MANUFACTURED IN CHINA
10 9 8 7 6 5 4 3 2
2020 Golden Books Edition

Peppa Pig is wearing a colorful Easter outfit.
Design another Easter outfit for Peppa to wear.

Daddy Pig has a basket full of Easter eggs to hide.
Can you find the small picture of Daddy Pig
that matches the big one?

Use the code to find out who has found some eggs.

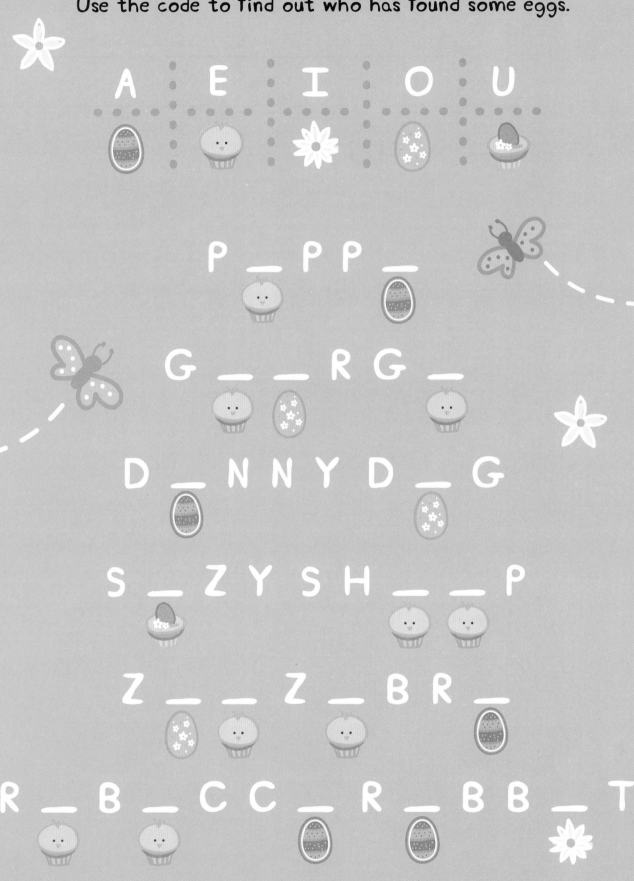

A   E   I   O   U

P _ P P _

G _ _ R G _

D _ N N Y D _ G

S _ Z Y S H _ _ P

Z _ _ _ Z _ B R _

R _ B _ C C _ R _ B B _ T

Answers on page 47

Peppa and her friends have to find the Easter egg
that matches their outfit.
Can you help them?

Answers on page 47

Peppa finds an egg hidden in a bush.
Use your stickers to add more eggs to the scene.

Find the missing puzzle pieces to see these springtime birds in their nest.

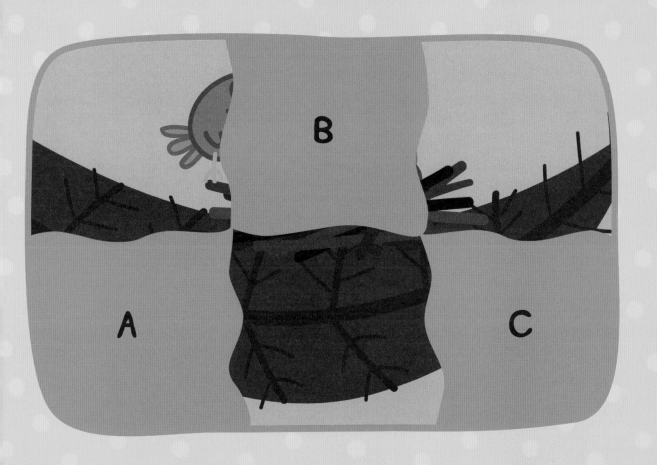

1

2

3

Answers on page 47

Mummy Pig has baked Easter cookies.
Draw some more treats for Peppa and her friends.

Peppa and her friends have found lots of Easter eggs.
How many can you count?

I count ____ eggs.

Answers on page 47

Egg-cellent Fun!
(A game for two players)

Taking turns with a friend, draw one line between two dots.
If you complete a box, write your initials in it and give yourself
one point. Give yourself two points if the box contains an
Easter egg. Whoever has more points at the end of the game wins!

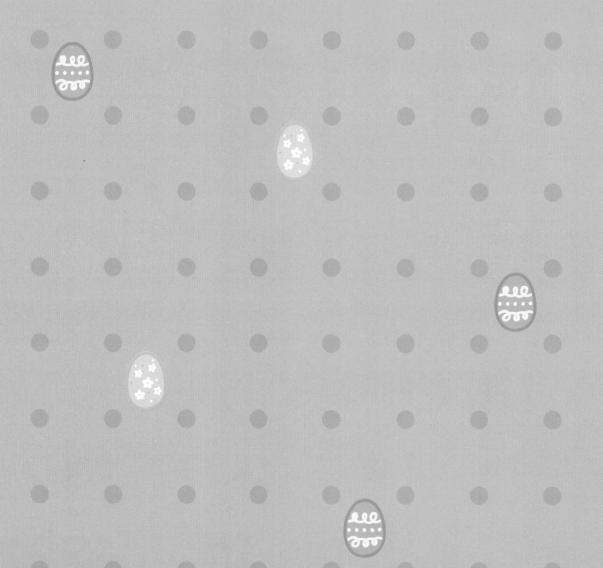

Play again!

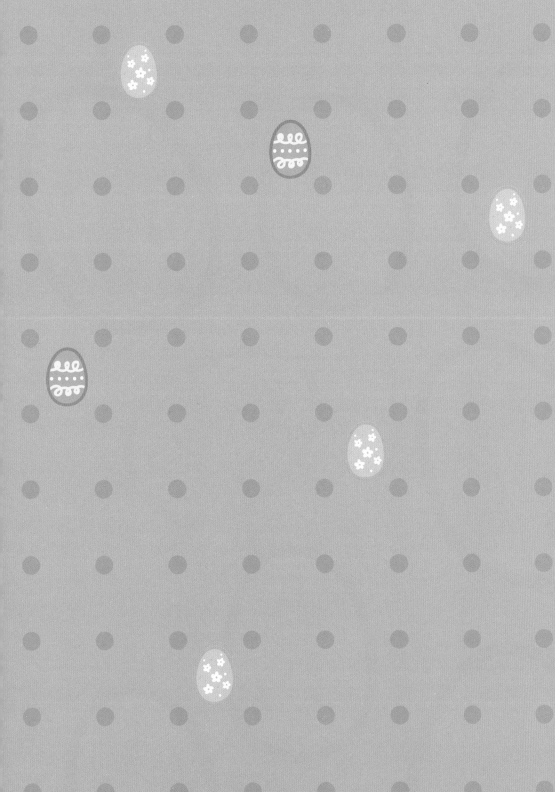

Help Peppa and George color the Easter eggs.

Look at the patterns. Figure out what the next duck in each row should be, and use your stickers to complete them.

1.

2.

3.

Answers on page 47

Help Peppa get to George and their picnic in the park.

START

FINISH

Answers on page 47

Peppa and her friends can't wait for a visit from the Easter Bunny!
Can you spot the five differences between the two pictures?

Answers on page 47

Peppa and George like to play tic-tac-toe.
Use your stickers to play with a friend.

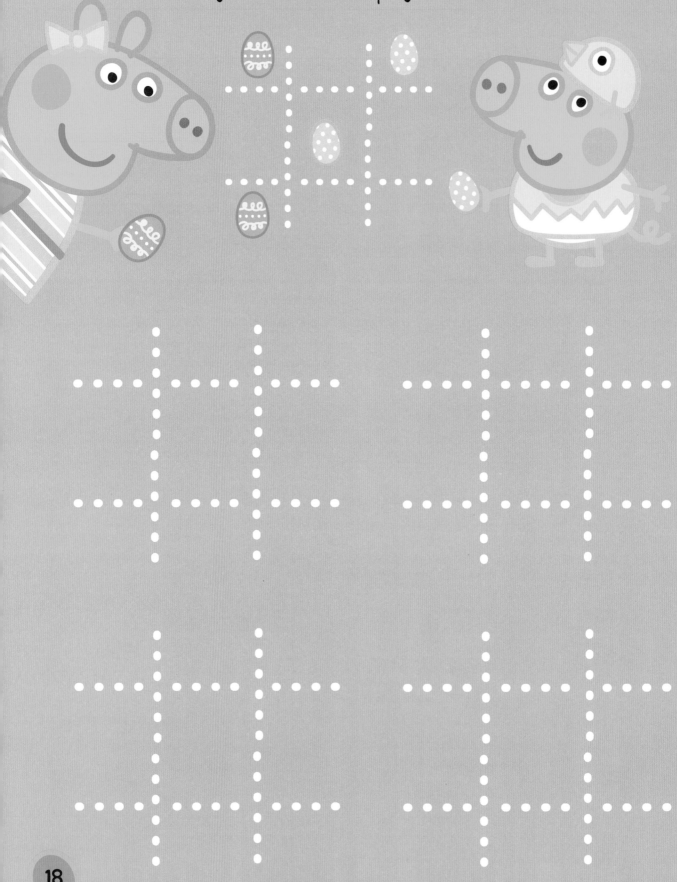

Connect the dots to see George's fluttery friend.

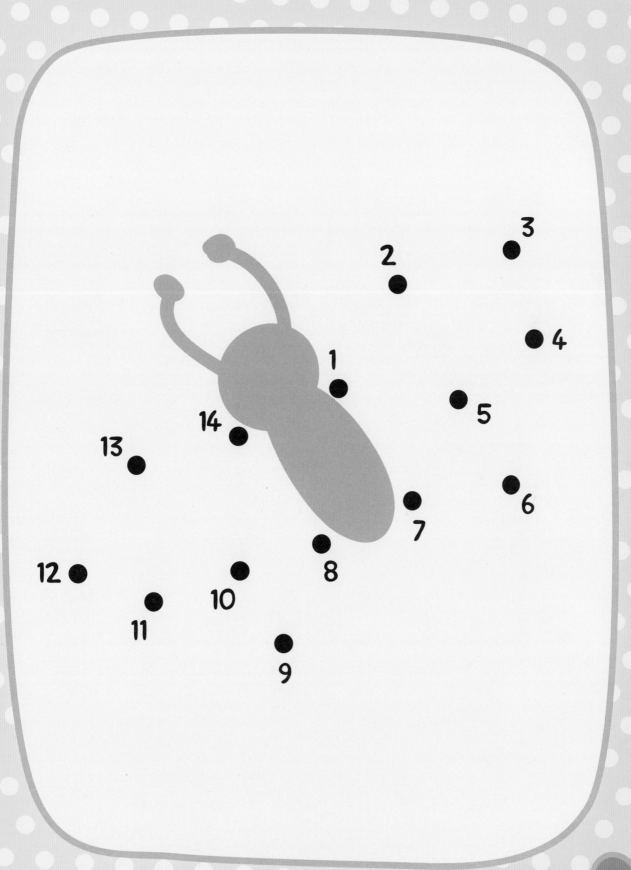

Answers on page 47

Look closely at those ears to figure out who is hiding in the bush.
Circle the correct one.

Answers on page 47

Use the key below to make George more colorful.

KEY
1 = yellow
2 = pink
3 = orange
4 = white

How many Easter eggs can you count in this basket?

I count _____ eggs.

Answers on page 47

Egg-cellent Fun

hoppy easter!

YUM YUMMY YUM!

Eggs this way

Hop to it!

Peppa is dressed like an Easter bunny.
Draw bunny ears on her head.

Circle the row of Easter eggs that is different from the rest.

A

B

C

D

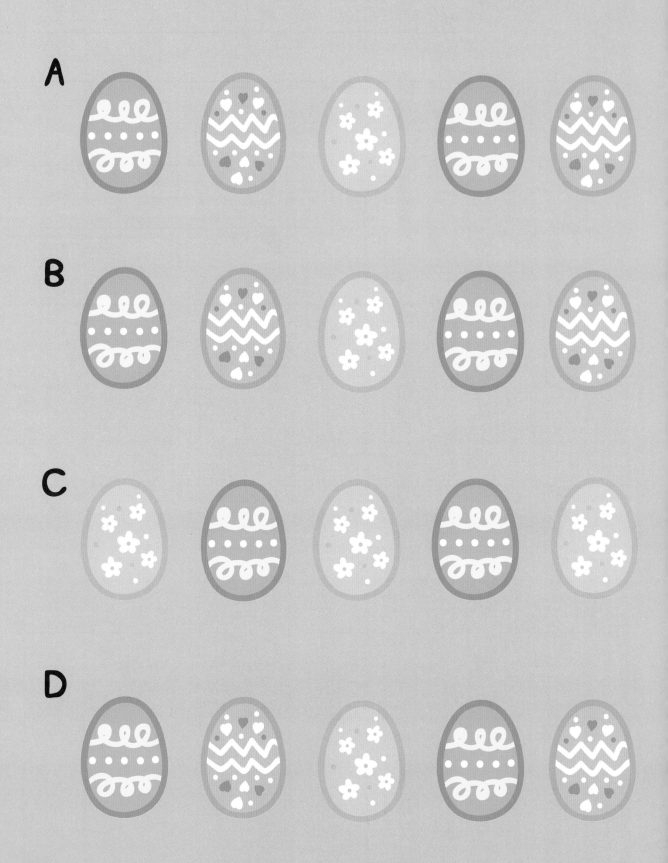

Answers on page 48

These little chicks are playing hide-and-seek.
How many chicks can you find?
Circle them.

Answers on page 48

Use your stickers to help Peppa and George add lots of flowers to Granny Pig's garden to celebrate spring.

Draw a big muddy puddle for Peppa and Zoe to jump in!

Match these shadows to their stickers so Peppa and her friends can go on an Easter egg hunt.

Some flying friends have come to visit Grandpa Pig's garden. Can you find the dragonfly that is different from the rest?

Answers on page 48

Uh-oh! Peppa and George have mixed the paints.
Do you know what colors you get by mixing the colors below?

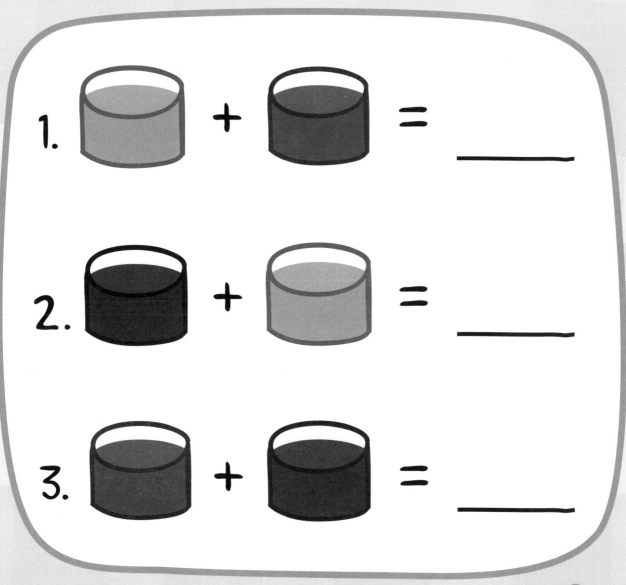

1. ⬜ + ⬛ = _____

2. ⬛ + ⬜ = _____

3. ⬛ + ⬛ = _____

Answers on page 48

Circle the Peppa that is different from the rest.

Answers on page 48

How many carrots can you count in Grandpa Pig's garden?

I count ____ carrots.

George has painted an Easter picture.
Now you draw a picture.
Use your stickers to add to the fun.

Mrs. Rabbit is looking for Rebecca and Peppa.
Help her by choosing the correct path to follow.

A

B

C

Answers on page 48

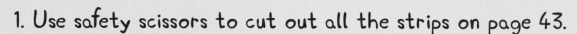

Flower Chain!

1. Use safety scissors to cut out all the strips on page 43.

2. Tape or glue the ends of one strip together to form a circle.

3. Thread the next strip through the circle, and tape or glue it to make another link in your chain.

4. Repeat until all the strips but one have been used.

5. Thread the last link through the first one to complete the circle.

6. Wear the chain as a crown or necklace to celebrate springtime!

ANSWERS

Page 3

Page 4

P E P P A

G E O R G E

D A N N Y D O G

S U Z Y S H E E P

Z O E Z E B R A

R E B E C C A R A B B I T

Page 5

Page 7

1 - B

2 - C

3 - A

Page 9

I count __7__ eggs.

Page 15

1.

2.

3.

Page 16

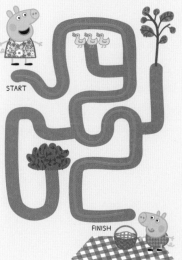

Page 17

Page 19

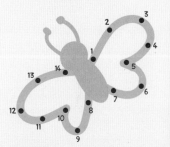

Page 20

Page 22

I count __6__ eggs.

ANSWERS

Page 26
Row C

Page 27

Page 34

Page 37
1. Orange
2. Green
3. Purple

Page 38

Page 39
I count __21__ carrots.

Page 41
Path C

Egg-citing Egg Holders!

Directions:

1. Carefully punch out an egg holder.
2. Form a ring and overlap the ends about 1 inch.
3. Tape the ends together.
4. Use your stickers to decorate the egg holder.
5. Carefully place your egg inside.
6. Repeat with the rest of the egg holders.

Happy Easter!

TO: _____

FROM: _____

Happy Easter!

TO: _____

FROM: _____

Happy Easter!

TO: _____

FROM: _____

Happy Easter!

TO: _____

FROM: _____

Some-bunny

loves you!

happy easter!

Have an egg-cellent

Easter!

Hello

spring!

You are egg-stra

special!

HAPPY SPRING TIME!

Hoppy Easter

HOP

Happy Easter!

TO: _____

FROM: _____

Happy Easter!

TO: _____

FROM: _____

Happy Easter!

TO: _____

FROM: _____

Happy Easter!

TO: _____

FROM: _____